Aztec Mythology

The Gods and Myths of
Ancient Mexico

Table of Contents

Introduction

The distinctive set of customs possessed and portrayed by different tribes, cultural groups, and religious clans extract their essence from different versions of their mythology. The tools we use, the food we eat, the beliefs we hold on to, and the clothes we wear are all ingredients influenced by myths, legends, and folk tales that collectively define mythology. In a way, our mythologies have revolutionized the world we live in and continue to impact us to date. The impact made by certain mythologies is heavier than others. One such set of beliefs belonged to the Aztecs.

Aztec mythology contains one of the strongest and most impactful tales of the beginning of the world and the existence of gods. This mythology has heavily jolted the Aztecs into framing a fixed set of beliefs and following certain rituals. Some of the mythological implications also set them apart from other communities and provide a distinct identity. For instance, they conducted human sacrifices and built a city based on their myths.

The Aztec civilization of Central Mexico consisted of several communities with distinct cultures and languages. The Nahuatl-speaking tribes were the most popular and celebrated rituals based on their own version of myths and stories. While the Mesoamerican cultures shared many stories, rituals, and myths with the Aztecs, they were recognized as a separate community. The Aztecs were believed to come from the regions around Lake Texcoco and the Anahuac Valley. These regions collectively form the modern Mexico City we know today. Since various versions and tales surround the Aztecs, this civilization's provenance can be narrowed down to these regions.

The Aztecs governed these regions during the 15th, 16th, and 17th centuries, regions referred to as Central Mexico today. The word "Aztec" means "one who belongs to or comes from Aztlán" in the Nahuatl language. However, the tribe preferred to call themselves Tenochca, Mexica, or Tlatelolco. "Azteca" is, in fact, a modern term that was coined by scholars in the 18th and 19th centuries to refer to a group of people residing in the Mexica state. Since they shared the same language, customs, religion, and trade, they were collectively known as the Aztecs. They spoke the Nahuatl language, which still exists today in certain communities. In fact, people of these communities identify as modern-day Aztecs.

Aztec mythology raises multiple questions yet keeps a reader engrossed. Certain definitions and subjects are alarming and can stir up a myriad of emotions in a modern-day man. Some bloody rituals included sacrificing humans and animals to the gods, self-sacrificing by cutting body parts, and cannibalism. It is also believed that multiple slaves and their children were sold off with plots of land to the rich. Despite these adversities, the creation tale, creativity, and agricultural implications stemming from Aztec mythology are extremely impressive and carried forward.

The myths also cover the relationships between important gods, goddesses and mystical creatures. In fact, the idea of creation carried by Aztec mythology is quite tenacious and portrays the participation of all deities at every stage. Even though several versions of the creation myth exist, one can pick the nitty-gritty to paint a picture.

Furthermore, the Aztecs were an isolated group and survived without depending on the Asian and European cultures of that time. They grew exponentially and developed a massive community with millions of people. With time, they drew parallels between distinct domains and showed progress in the fields of agriculture, economy, transportation, arts, and architecture.

In this book, we will cover the distinct nuances of Aztec mythology, its deities, creatures, interesting folk tales, rituals, religious celebrations, and the beliefs held by the community. Every aspect of the Aztecs' livelihood was governed by their myths and beliefs, which is why it is necessary to dig deep and understand the crux of their version of mythology.

Read on to grasp the entirety of Aztec mythology and comprehend the hidden tales and folklore that most people are unaware of.

Chapter 1:

Aztec Deities

J ust like all tribes and cultures, the Aztecs have their own deities and believe in supreme souls. The Aztecs defined their gods and goddesses based on distinct symbols and roles. While there were several gods, goddesses, and deities that the Aztecs believed in, ten of them were especially of high standing and were supremely worshipped and signified.

Huitzilopochtli – "The Hummingbird of the South"

Pronunciation: Weetz-ee-loh-POSHT-lee

Commonly known as the Father of the Aztecs or the Patron, Huitzilopochtli was the primary messenger or well-wisher of the Aztecs when they were shifting their base from Aztlan (their original home) to the capital city of Tenochtitlan. He guided the Aztecs throughout their migration phase and directed them on the right path. He was also often referred to as "the Hummingbird of the Left. "This is the literal translation of his name, with the eagle being his spirit animal. However, his relevance to earlier Mesoamerican cultures is still unknown and ambiguous.

The Patron of war, sacrifice, and the sun, Huitzilopochtli's shrine was constructed atop Templo Mayor, a prevalent pyramid in Tenochtitlan. The structure was decorated with red paint to signify blood and adorned with skulls. It is believed that Coyolxauhqui, the Goddess of Moon, was Huitzilopochtli's sibling, and both were rivals, as demonstrated by the well-known tiffs between the Sun and Moon to take over the sky. The fallen warrior and their spirits were known to escort the Patron at crucial steps. These spirits were believed to belong to women who died young and the ones that would fall on earth as hummingbirds.

Quetzalcoatl – "The Feathered Serpent"

Pronunciation: Keh-tzal-coh-atl

This deity has several names and forms in varied arenas of Aztec myths and beliefs. While he was primarily known as Quetzalcoatl in the Aztec community, Mesoamerican cultures, especially the Maya and Teotihuacan, recognized him by other titles and regarded him as a significant god. He was well-known for his creativity, immense knowledge, and learning capacity. Moreover, he was praised for his ability to practice self-reflection. His name was derived from two Nahuatl words- "quetzal," meaning the bird with the emerald, and "coatl," meaning serpent. Thereby, the name indicated the involvement of two living creatures- a rattlesnake and a bird.

Quetzalcoatl was often associated with the planet Venus and was believed to have invented books. Furthermore, the Aztecs also linked the invention of calendars to this God. Once, Quetzalcoatl descended on earth with his companion Xolotl, a dog-headed being. Upon descending, the God and his companion went on a quest to search for bones belonging to the ancient dead, gathering as many as they could. These bones were then infused with Quetzalcoatl's own blood and bones to create life and regenerate the population from scratch. Moctezuma, the last emperor of the Aztecs, believed that Quetzalcoatl's return was a prophecy fulfilled by the Spanish conqueror Cortes.

Tezcatlipoca – "The Smoking Mirror"

Pronunciation: Tez-cah-tlee-poh-ka

The God of Night, Tezcatlipoca, was linked to the cold, evil energies, and death. His sibling, Quetzalcoatl, led his people with a noble cause and created life, which completely contradicted Tezcatlipoca's ways. He ruled the north and was known as the ruler of the night. His evil intentions were well-known, which also gave him a negative reputation. His image is perceived as a figure with a black-striped face and is believed to hold an obsidian mirror. Since his name refers to a "smoking mirror" in Nahuatl, he was always linked with the mirror. Tezcatlipoca was also known by other names such as the God of time, ancestral memory, and the nocturnal sky.

Even though Tezcatlipoca was believed to be the evil God, myths claim that he actively participated with his brother Huitzilopochtli in creating the world. While Huitzilopochtli helped the people and acted as a positive force to guide those on the land, Tezcatlipoca represented cold and death, which were inevitable. Among all tribes, the Toltecs (a warrior tribe from the north who speak Nahua as their main language) worshipped this God and considered him a supreme deity. Myths say that his nagual or spirit guardian was the jaguar.

Tonatiuh – "The Turquoise Lord"

Pronunciation: Toh-nah-tee-uh

Tonatiuh was the God of the Sun and the Lord of nourishment. He could provide fertile lands and food to his people. He was also known to give warmth and keep the inhabitants insulated from cold. However, his nourishing power came from sacrificial blood, which meant the incessant death of living beings. He ruled the Aztec era (also known as the period of the Fifth Sun) when the tribe actually witnessed the happenings. Since he was the Patron of all warriors, Tonatiuh led the tribes with pride and provided the necessary resources for them to survive.

The popular illustration inscribed on the Aztec sunstone displays Tonatiuh in the center. He is also represented by a sun disk that is symbolic in nature.

Other illustrations portray him as a man carrying a disk on his back in a squatted position. As mentioned, he was associated with the ritual of sacrificing blood, which is avidly covered in the cultural stories of the post-classic Mesoamerican habitants. According to them, the victims' hearts were illustrated as the sun's source of nourishment. With these sacrifices, Tonatiuh could defeat darkness and gain nourishment.

Chalchiuhtlicue – "She Who Wears a Green Skirt"

Pronunciation: Tchal-chee-uh-tlee-ku-eh

Better known as the Goddess of Running Water, this deity represented aquatic elements and flowing water. "She who wears a green skirt" or "she of the Jade Skirt" is the literal translation of her name. The flowing skirt represents running water, and the bluish-green hues depict its color. Known to be the patroness of childbirth and Tlaloc's sister or wife, Chalchiuhtlicue was also linked to serpents and related symbols. She was the primary protector of newborns and would go out of her way to protect them.

In certain versions of the deluge myth (particularly the Mexica version), she was worshipped as the main God. Even though she was responsible for bringing a heavy flood that caused a calamity, she saved humans by transforming them into fish. In some cultures, the Goddess was celebrated by following certain rituals such as feasting, sacrificing humans, fasting, and bloodletting. Some cultures also defined the Goddess as a prime navigator who led others on the right path. Her home was embedded deep in the mountains, and she released water as she deemed fit, which irrigated the streams flowing through the valleys.

Coatlicue – "The Serpent Skirt"

Pronunciation: Kow-tli-hkyuw

This feminine God was known to be the mother of the mortals and other gods. Several myths claim that she produced the moon and the stars, which makes her the mother of these celestial bodies as well. Her face was made up of two serpents with fangs, which is why she was closely associated with the symbol of serpents. Her dress was made of interwoven snakes with skulls, hearts, and hands as her jewelry. Even though she was a beloved god, she was feared by the people due to her demeanor.

The contraction between childbirth and earth worship was drawn due to this God's presence. Other areas of supreme rule included agriculture, governance, and welfare and Coatepec, a sacred mountain of the era, held a legendary shrine. Myths say that Coatlicue often visited this site to sweep the structure. Once when she was at the shrine sweeping, she saw a mysterious ball of feathers swiftly falling down from the sky, which later impregnated the God. As a result, the God of war, Huitzilopocht-li, was born. However, the god's sons, the Centzon Huitznahua, and daughter, Coyolxauhqui, were outraged and embarrassed by this and decided to kill their mother after climbing Mt. Coatepec.

Centeotl - "Maize Cob Lord"

Pronunciation: Cen-teh-otl

Venerated as The God of Maize, Centeotl was a pan-Mesoamerican god worshipped by multiple tribes, especially the Maya and Olmec religions. As the name suggests, the Maize cob Lord was repre-sented by a maize cob that diligently sprouted from the god's headdress. This God was significant to some tribes as they believed him to be the source of reproduction, life, and agriculture. While some perceived Centeotl to be masculine, others believed him to have feminine characteristics. In some tales, this God was believed to be born a female and later acquired masculine traits to become Centeotl, the Maize cob Lord with Chicomecoátl as his feminine counterpart.

Centeotl was the child of Tlazolteotl (the Goddess of childbirth and fertility) and Xochipilli. Both Chicomecoátl and Centeotl supervised the stages of maturation and ensured access of maize to all parts. According to a popular myth, Centeotl gathered several food items when he visited the underworld, including sweet potatoes, cotton, pulque, or octli (an agave drink that intoxicated people), and huauzontle. He gave these items to humans, which is one of the reasons he is linked to the morning star, Venus.

Xipe Totec – "Our Lord the Flayed One"

Pronunciation: Shee-peh Toh-tek

The God of Fertility and Sacrifice, Xipe Totec, was the deity of the goldsmiths and agricultural fertility. He also ruled over the east and ensured peace among the inhabitants of that region. Xipe Totec's popular title "Our Lord with the flayed skin" comes from his ensemble, comprising a dress made of flayed human skin. This dress symbolized the end of the old and made room for new growth and vegetation. The god's brutal act of slaying his own skin to provide food to the humans is the reason behind his gruesome name.

Xipe Totec is remembered during the popular festival Tlacaxipehualiztli, usually held in March. The word refers to the act of flaying men, which is how the god is venerated. Every human caught doing wrong was imprisoned and later flayed during this festival. He was given a wooden club with blades, known as a macuahuitl, along with a stone. Instead of knives, the tool was designed using feathers. As the procession was carried out, the prisoner was placed in front of an Aztec warrior in a duel. Certain re-enactors of the God would then wear the prisoner's flayed skin. Later on, the re-enactors were killed too. The Aztec priests were provided with their flayed skins and hearts. Once the first 20 days passed, the ritual of shedding the skin took place, marking the rebirth or reincarnation of Xipe Totec.

Tlaloc – "He Who Makes Things Sprout"

Pronunciation: Tláh-lock

The God of Rain and Storms, Tlaloc, was one of the oldest gods and was worshipped by ancient civilizations such as the Olmec, the Teotihuacan, and the Maya. In fact, all of Mesoamerica and its surrounding regions knew and worshipped Tlaloc. He was the symbol of agriculture, fertility, and growth. The Templo Mayor held another shrine that was dedicated to this God. Since he was the representative of agriculture and growth, his shrine was adorned with blue bands to depict water and rain. In some cultures, the association between the god's sacredness and the cries of newborns was discreet, which is why newborn children were often sacrificed as a tribute to Tlaloc.

The god's ensemble comprised a huge mask with fangs and huge eyes. He was often compared with the Maya rain god, Chac, due to the similarity in their looks. While Tlaloc was immensely generous as he provided rain and crops to the humans on the land, he was also feared due to his destructive nature. He would often send droughts, floods, and storms when he was angry. This unforgiving nature threw fear into the hearts of the people. This is also why many believed him to be the ruler of Thalocan, the other-worldly land filled with diseases, storms, and undesirable phenomena.

Mayahuel - "The Woman of the 400 Breasts"

Pronunciation: My-ya-whale

Commonly known as the Goddess of Maguey, Mayahuel was the representative of the maguey plant. She was given the title "the woman of the 400 breasts" due to her nourishing and feeding nature. She always provided food to her children and en-sured that everyone had food on their plates. Her common powers included revitalization and fer-tility. Drunkenness and Maguey were her realms. The reference to her many breasts also relates to the multiple maguey leaves and sprouts. Moreover, the plants produce some form of milky juice which bears a resemblance to the nutrition and food pro-vided by mothers through their breasts.

The title is also associated with the "400 rabbits" or the Centzon Totochtin, the gods who drank excessively. Mayahuel is illustrated as a woman rising above a maguey plant, holding the foamed plaque in multiple cups. She appears in the Codex Borbonicus dressed in blue clothing and wearing a headdress decorated with multiple spindles. The blue hues represent fertility and growth, which Mayahuel symbolizes. Furthermore, the headdress is also shown with ixtle or raw maguey fiber. Some illustrations even depict the Goddess seated on a maguey plant with a gourd.

Chapter 2:

Aztec Creatures

While the Gods and Goddesses of the Aztecs were immensely popular and even worshipped in distant lands, the creatures were also frequently mentioned in the Aztec folklore. Most of these creatures were strange and bore superpowers. While some possessed purely animalistic traits, others were a hybrid of spirits, animals, or humans. This is partly why some of the creatures were referred to as "monsters" of the Aztec community. From shape-shifting monsters to lake creatures, Aztec mythology covers a myriad of interesting figures, some of which we will discuss in this chapter.

Nahual

The word "Nahual" translates to "hidden disguise" in the Nahuatl language and refers to a creature that can shape-shift into different forms, all of them being animals. He is known as a famous sorcerer who possesses witchcraft abilities, which is how he transforms into different animals. It is believed that all humans are born with distinct animal spirits or Nahual, which guides and protects them. However, if one is unable to discover the hidden potential of their Nahual, the spirit guide will not be able to guide them. That being said, every human has a different nahual or spirit animal, which defines their intuition and primary traits.

For example, if your spirit animal is a wolf, you may have an enhanced sense of smell. On the other hand, individuals with a hawk as their spirit guide may have better sight. In the past, it was believed that the living beings who got to use their nahual powers could easily achieve their goals. It didn't matter if the purpose was evil or noble; they just needed to unleash their power. Myths and stories related to Nahuals are different and distinct across various cultures, which often impact the perception of these mysterious creatures.

Atotolin

Aztec culture's Bird King, Atotolin, was a water hen with a large yellow head and a slender body. Hunters would often seek these birds and go on quests to search for them. However, finding an Atotolin was not an easy feat. If the hunters failed to find and hunt the bird by the fourth day, they would feel strong winds and hear a song in the background. The hearts of the hunters would then stop due to the strong winds that were capable of sinking boats and canoes. As the winds would get stronger and the water would rise, the hunters would drown and die.

If any hunter got lucky and could find the bird, they would rip its stomach apart to know their fate. In most cases, they would find some kind of object that would dictate their future and fate. For instance, a piece of precious stone would bless the hunter with a prosperous life. On the other hand, a piece of coal could mean an early death for the hunter. Some illustrations depict this bird with a blue, slender body with a redhead and bright yellow beak. The colorful hues of the bird made it an interesting and popular Aztec creature.

Cipactli

The word "Cipactli" translates to "black lizard." This creature was half-crocodile, half-fish, and possessed peculiar features that are difficult to describe. With 18 mouths and a voracious body, the creature was always hungry and sought food through hunting. To capture his bait, the Cipactli used his feet to bring them closer. Some illustrations even depict the creature with feet that resemble a frog's. He was ideally perceived as a sea monster with body parts resembling various aquatic animals. The many mouths were located in specific locations of the creature's arms and legs. It is believed that heaven and earth were inspired by and created with the help of Cipactli's body.

In some cultures, this creature also represented the beginning of life and new eras, which is why it is often illustrated on the first page of calendars. It also signifies that all living beings are primitive until they grow and transform over time. If they take the right path and find their true calling, they can transform into an exceptional soul and become beautiful. This also explains the illustration of Xochitl on the last page of the calendar, which means "flower" and indicates transformation.

Tlahuelpuchi

This word translates to "light perfumer" and is often referred to as Tlatlepuchi. This creature has been a popular figure in Mexican folk tales and is famous in many regions. The prominent form of this creature is illustrated as a woman who possesses telepathic powers and hunts living beings to feed on their blood. Even though she would hunt animals of all sizes, she specifically preferred the blood of smaller animals. While some claim this woman to be a mix of vampire and sorceress, others see her as a witch. She was believed to have transformative powers and could use magic to turn into steam.

Some myths also claim that this creature exists in the form of men as well, which are called Tlahuelpiches. Both genders are believed to thrive with fireflies, particularly the ones that spit or omit fire. Some legends even claim that these creatures were noble but turned evil due to a spell or curse. In some cultures, the Tlatlepuchi is believed to thrive among commoners but may not hurt them or their families. In some cases, they might also live alone without facing the public. The Tlatlepuchi only get their powers when they reach adolescence.

Ahuitzotl

All tribes feared this dog-like creature due to its hideous appearance and ability to manipulate others. This creature would also often hunt humans and feed on their flesh. It would target certain parts, such as the eyes, nails, and teeth, making it scarier. Ahuiztol's tail had an additional hand that enabled it to catch its prey. It was always found near or inside water bodies. Its name literally translates to "spiny aquatic creature," which resonates with "water dog." Its manipulative and luring powers would attract humans towards it, making it easier for Ahuitzotl to snatch them with the hand on its tail.

As soon as the creature left the water, its fur would spike, and its hands would become active. Some myths claim that the Ahuiztol was the guardian of certain aquatic bodies, especially the lakes. It would stay in the water when it's not hunting and protect all fish. A few versions tell the story of how the Ahuiztol was the pawn of Chalchiuhtlicue and Tlaloc and how they sent him to the earth to lure humans and collect their souls. Some tales also mention sightings of the creature in and near Lake Texcoco. If the creature got extremely hungry or failed to catch any prey for a while, it would let out a screaming cry that sounded like a baby's wail.

Chaneque

Commonly known as Chanekeh or Ohuican Chaneque, this creature was a dainty-looking sprite with drooping ears and child-like characteristics. Its name in Nahuatl translates to "owners of the house" or "those who inhabit dangerous places." These creatures were believed to be the guardians of the mountains and the animals that lived there. Some Chaneques were even known to exist deep in the forests, where they took care of wild animals, trees, and springs. This is why they were called the ultimate guardians of nature. They would look for humans and scare them to let their souls out. If they managed to catch any soul, they would dig a deep hole and bury it inside the land.

The victims still had the chance to revive their soul and bring it back into their bodies through certain rituals. If they failed to do so, they would die due to sickness. The peculiar characteristics of these tiny beings made them look like children, with the facial features of older women and men. This gave rise to the superstition of wearing clothes backward to distract the Chaneques and keep them from taking your soul. Their behavioral traits resembled those of a child. They would throw stones, pull tails, break things, and engage in mischievous behavior.

Tzitzimitl

One of the most feared creatures in Aztec mythology, the Tzitzimitl is represented by a skeleton that is ornamented with crossbones designs and skirts. Their queen, Itzpapalotl, ruled Tamoanchan, the paradise of the Tzitzimime. It was believed that the Tzitzimitl were closely associated with the stars, particularly those roaming around the sun during the eclipse. Even though they looked evil, they did not necessarily represent evil forces. However, different versions of the tales depict different connotations. It is apparent from their appearance that the Tzitzimitl were female and represented fertility. This is why parturient women and midwives worshipped these deities.

Their relation to the solar eclipse forged the belief of the Tzitzimitl attacking humans and possessing men during this period. Their possession and defense were entirely dependent on the 52-year calendar round and their ability to hit the chest cavity with a bow fire. While men feared the arrival of these creatures during the solar eclipse, some creatures would even attack during New Year. The tales, depiction, and mentions of the Tzitzimitl became so popular due to the folklore being referenced in pop culture, especially in movies and books.

The Centzon Mimixcoa (Four-Hundred Cloud Serpents)

These creatures were associated with the northern stars and believed to be the sons of the Earth Goddess, Coatlicue, and Camaxtle-Mixcoatl. Other versions claim them to be the sons of the Goddess of the seas, Chalchiuhtlicue and Tonatiuh. According to a script, the four-hundred cloud serpents were segregated into five types after transforming into stars. Those types are Tlo-tepētl ("Hawk Mountain"), Cuāuhtli-icohuauh ("Eagle's Twin"), Cuetlach-cihuatl, (the sister- "hid in the ball court"), Apan-teutli ("River Lord"), and Mix-cōātl ("Cloud Serpent"). These protagonists were forced to sacrifice themselves to Tonatiuh, the Sun god. However, they promptly refused and neglected their responsibilities.

According to legends, they were the siblings of Mixcoatl who fought them due to negligence. Their irresponsibility caused a cosmic imbalance, which triggered Mixocatl to take them down. While the laxity of the brothers was the main reason for the tiff, Mixcoatl also grew greedy and wished to abuse his powers. However, he had to wait for all his brothers to transform and turn into cloud serpents. It is believed that these creatures populated the land when Camaxtle hit a rock with a cane. This was even before the Aztecs existed.

The Centzon Totochtin (Four-Hundred Rabbits)

Popularly known as the Gods of Drunkenness, these creatures held bunny-like characteristics and were believed to be the sons of the Goddess of pulque, Mayahuel. Even though they are often referred to as a group of four hundred rabbits, the context implies they were innumerable. They lived in harmony and rarely got into tiffs. Unlike other creatures that were frequently involved in fights and battles with the gods and demigods, the Centzon Totochtin preferred to stay away from any sort of commotion. However, certain things did agitate the little creatures. They were believed to be alcoholics and could attack or hurt others due to alcoholism. Unable to handle the amount of alcohol they consumed, they were feared by others when spotted with intoxicating liquids.

If someone threatened or troubled the creatures under the influence, they would surely be killed or hurt. This gave birth to the popular saying, "drunk as 400 rabbits", which is said to someone who has had a lot of alcohol. Myths claim that the rabbits drank pulque, which, as mentioned, is the juice of maguey or fermented agave. According to myths, the main bunny gods were Macuil Tochtli – "Five Rabbit," Tepoztecatl (Ome Tochtli) – "Two Rabbit," Tequechmecauiani – "God of Hanging," Colhuatzincatl – "The Winged One," Techalotl – "God of Dance," Toltecatl – "God of Early Civilization," and Tezcatzoncatl – "The Straw Mirror."

Ixpuxtequi

Another feared creature of Aztec myths, Ixpuxtequi, was a monster that traveled during the night and hunted lonely people for food. Since travelers mostly commuted alone, he would take the same paths and kill them. His name translates to 'broken face' in the Nahuatl language, which describes his eerie demeanor and spooky silhouette. He was believed to have a broken jaw, which added to his intimidating persona. Normally, the creature would look like an abnormal humanoid figure due to his long legs, which resembled an eagle's. However, upon looking closer, travelers realized that he was missing the lower jaw. Those who escaped his grip would have nightmares for a prolonged period. In any way, those who saw him would be doomed for life.

He always carried a long staff that he would lean on when tired. Among the four deities of death, Ixpuxtequi was one of the most feared figures who did not show any mercy. He was known to be a symbol of a curse and brought misfortunes. Nexoxco, the Goddess of horror and fear, was known to be his wife and was equally scary. The God of mental illnesses and sleep disorders, Xoaltentli, was believed to be Ixpuxtequi's brother-in-law.

Chapter 3:

Creation Tale

E very version of Aztec mythology and folklore describes the creation tale with minor to major variations, primarily because the ancestors followed the oral tradition to pass down the stories from generation to generation. They named the tale "The Legend of the Fifth Sun." As the Aztecs conquered new regions, they renamed and changed their gods, which modified the creation myth as well. This caused differences in the stories and popularized various versions of the same tale.

The cycle of destruction and creation was at a spin in the Aztec civilization's fifth era, also when the Spanish conquered the region. This cultivated the belief that the world had been destroyed and recreated four times with the fifth cycle in progress. The world dramatically changed as different gods ruled during each cycle. Since every God had a distinctive way of ruling the world, they used a dominant element to stand apart, which produced different results. Collectively, the different worlds were named suns.

Before the World was Created

According to several myths, Tonacateuctli (god Ometeotl) and Tonacacihuatl were the creators that existed from the beginning. They gave birth to the Tezcatlipocas of the four directions, North, East, West, and South, also named Quetzalcoatl, Huitzilopochtli, Xipec Totec, and Tezcatlipoca. As they grew up and garnered knowledge of the world and the right way to rule the world, they started to create the universe after 600 years. The universe, the world, and cosmic time created were collectively called the "suns." Along with creating the world, the four sons also conceived the other deities. As time passed, they created humans. However, this would not have been possible if one of the gods did not sacrifice himself. The other gods needed him to jump into a fire before giving light to living beings.

With time, the gods decided to sacrifice themselves one by one to create the four suns. In turn, the Aztecs started to believe that sacrifice was needed for recreation or beginning new things, a thought that stuck around till now. The sacrificed God's blood dripped on a pile of bones, which, according to legends, belonged to the first woman and man, Cipactonal and Oxomoco. Once the gods created the first humans, they set out to create the rulers of the underworld, water, and skies. They also created Cipactli, a water monster resembling a dragon that floats over nothing (in the void). It was believed that our world and universe were stretched out, only until the extent of Cipactli's body. Anything and everything beyond its body blended into nothingness. Its body encompassed the thirteen heavens, the earth, and the nine underworlds in its head, torso, and tail, respectively, making Cipactli a giant that stretches beyond one's imagination. It contains the entire universe, celestial bodies, and living beings inside it. Myths say that the creature's body contained the earth in the form of a flat disc and was placed in the center of Celestial Waters, which is how our earth looks today.

One can reason with this belief by considering all four directions and cardinal points. If one starts moving towards the east direction and keeps walking for days, they will eventually reach the water. It is the same in all directions. However, this fact was conceived based on the earth being flat and shaped like a disc. Another interesting take on this inference is the belief that divides the earth into four quadrants, with the center being the navel. This is where Ometeotl resided and controlled the creation of the universe.

It is believed that the creator of the creators, Ometeotl was the sole power that existed over a prolonged period. Everything that was and everything that could have been was immersed in just one being. In these situations, the myths claim that opposite forces unite. Harmony and peace coexist with destruction and pessimism, which creates a peculiar balance. Since the Supreme Lord is the initiator of chaos and the one who restores order in the universe, he manifests power and is known as the God of Duality. In his presence, fire and water, good and evil, stillness and motion, matter and spirit, and black and white coexist.

This also gives him the power to give abundantly or take away everything at once. The supremacy of opposites converging in the same universe makes him divine. With time, the creation of himself-herself marked the beginning of life on earth. As mentioned, he resided in the navel or the center of the earth's quadrants, from where he controlled all entities. The extended directions from the center became the horizons, seas, water bodies, and the heavens. The four regions were therefore formed with their own distinct characteristics because of the sun's passage.

The Four Suns or the Four Cycles

As mentioned, the gods had to sacrifice themselves for the renewal of the worlds. Each of the four siblings took turns to govern each sun and decided their fates. When everything was void, and nothing existed (no breath, no life, no light, no motion, and no consciousness), Ometeotl took charge to change the course ahead. As you know, he portrayed both feminine and masculine features, which led him to create himself-herself. This gave birth to he-she, who took charge and began living. With this, the dark emptiness was filled with life, and nothing was replaced by everything.

The four siblings were also known as the ministers of Genesis and added visible changes to the physical and palpable world. They prevailed in the universe and took turns to govern each world. In a way, they were the guardians of all living beings, including humans, animals, and plants. They would supervise the living conditions and reward or punish according to their protocol.

First Sun

The first world, or the "4 Tiger," was created by the personal sacrifice of Tezcatlipoca (commonly called Black Tezcatlipoca) and lasted over 13 53-year cycles, which comprised a total of 676 years. It is believed that Huitzilopochtli and Quetzalcoatl were half sun and fire. They were also the gods who created the first sun and its constituents. Instead of humans, the first world was majorly occupied by animals and giants who needed acorns to eat and survive. They were then eaten by jaguars, which made their species extinct. Legends claim that Tezcatlipoca sent the jaguars to take revenge on Quetzalcoatl after they got into a fight. Eventually, the first sun came to an end. The element of the first sun was known to be earth.

Second Sun

The second sun was popularly known as the "4-Wind" sun and lasted the same duration as the first world, 676 years. It was created and ruled by Quetzalcoatl (commonly called White Tezcatlipoca). Even though this sun was occupied by humans (unlike the first world), they possessed peculiar features as opposed to humans today. They were noble, kind, and unlike the corrupt humans of today. However, with time, they did become corrupt.

They survived on pinon nuts and turned into monkeys when catastrophic disasters struck the land. Deadly floods and hurricanes killed most of the humans, and the rest survived after fleeing to the treetops and transforming into animals. Legends say that the corrupt nature of humans led Tezcatlipoca to wipe them out and order Quetzalcoatl to send floods and hurricanes. The monkeys that survived the calamities are believed to be the ancestors of the apes that are present to date. The calamities and natural disasters eventually destroyed the second sun. The element of the second sun was known to be air.

Third Sun

Tlaloc, the rain god, was the main creator and ruler of the third world or the "4-Rain" sun. This world was governed by the water element, which provided food to the living beings. The third sun lasted just 364 years, which is around 7 cycles. The story revolved around the fight between Tlaloc and Tezcatlipoca when the latter kidnapped Tlaloc's wife. Humans extracted seeds from the water to feed on and quenched their thirst by drinking them from natural water bodies. However, Quetzalcoatl was angered due to Tezcatlipoca's sin and dried the water by sending fire and ashes to the world. Those who survived transformed into different animals, namely dogs, butterflies, and turkeys. Some myths claim that Tlaloc was the reason why humans transformed into animals. The element of the second sun was known to be fire.

Fourth Sun

The fourth sun lasted longer, around 676 years (just like the first and second worlds). It was governed by Tlaloc's sister and wife, goddess Chalchiuthlicue. Humans of this world survived on maize as it was abundant during the fourth Sun. Just like the third Sun, the fourth world was also destroyed due to a catastrophic flood that ended all living beings. Those who survived turned into fishes and survived the flood. Legends say that the destruction happened due to the jealousy of Tezcatlipoca and Quetzalcoatl as they wanted to annihilate the main God's presence. The element of the second sun was known to be water.

The New World-The Fifth Sun

As the fourth world ended, the universe and cosmic elements were pushed into a void, which resulted in utter darkness. As the time arrived for the creation of the fifth sun, all the gods gathered to make a decision regarding the sacrifice. However, all the gods were hesitant when the old fire god, Huehueteotl, lit a bonfire and asked any one of them to jump. The Lord of Snails, Tecuciztecatl, was the most hesitant of all the gods, as he was proud and rich. In the end, Nanahuatzin sacrificed himself by spontaneously jumping into the fire during the argument. However, Tecuciztecatl felt guilty and remorseful, which led him to jump into the fire too. Due to this, the fifth world would collectively be ruled by two suns.

Upon realizing the major chaos and imbalance this would create, the other gods sacrificed a rabbit by throwing it on Tecuciztecatl, which gave birth to the moon. According to some old and new tales, the rabbit appears on the moon due to this incident. This is also why we have one sun and one moon today. Later, the God of the wind, Ehecatl, helped the celestial bodies to move and set them in motion by heavily blowing on the sun.

Referred to as the "4-Movement", the sun god, Tonatiuh, currently rules the fifth world. The significance of the motion is associated with the day sign, Ollin, which is linked to movement. As the end is near, the world will be destroyed by another natural calamity (plausibly earthquakes). Myths say that the fifth world will likely end due to the invasion of sky monsters as well. According to some tales, the Aztecs are obliged to conduct sacrifices and offerings to the Sun god to keep him nourished. If they fail to follow this duty, they will suffer from eternal darkness as the Sun god will disappear, which will also cause the world to end.

The Legend of the Fifth Sun is one of the most popular creation stories among all versions. According to the Aztecs, we are currently living in the fifth sun, and it is extremely difficult to predict its end. The Aztec Calendar Stone carries an inscription of one of the popular versions of this creation tale.

End of the Calendar Cycle

As you learned, each cycle ends at a 52-year mark, which is when the Aztec religious leaders and priests performed the New Fire Ceremony. This ritual was believed to bind the years together and await a better fate. Even though the five suns collectively predicted and marked the calendar cycle's end, they still couldn't decipher and mark the last cycle. Not knowing the exact phase of the end, the Aztecs started worshipping and following certain rituals to keep the gods pleased and experience a pleasant end. The rituals included de-cluttering the house, discarding cooking pots, mats, idols, clothing, and deep cleaning the house. At the end of the year, the last five days were spent extinguishing fires and gathering on the roof.

The religious leaders and priests would watch the Pleiades after climbing the Star Mountain (known as Cerro de la Estrella today). They would observe the star path and make sure that its direction and movement are intact. A victim was sacrificed each time, and their heart was placed in the fire drill to confirm the sun's longevity. Failing to light the fire after multiple tries indicated the destruction of the sun. If the priests were successful in lighting the fire, they would bring it to the city to renew lives and spread positive messages. Bernardo Sahagun, a famous Spanish chronicler, explains that the Aztecs held this ceremony across various villages once every 52 years.

One can draw parallels between the creation myth of the Aztecs and the texts inscribed by ancient Sumerians and Egyptians. Even though every story has its own perception and style of narration, they all mark the significance of God's role in creating and destroying living entities.

Chapter 4:

Myths and Stories

Aztec mythology is filled with numerous interesting tales that remain popular to this day. As you know, the Aztecs believed in sacrificing themselves and others to impress the gods and keep them happy. In fact, those chosen for sacrifice considered this act as an honor. Since the gods were always hungry, the Aztecs would provide goods, grains, animals, and humans as food. While some of the popular stories were about the deities and the sacrifices humans made for them, others had an interesting take on romance, poetry, trickery, and courage- some subjects that the Aztecs valued. In this chapter, we will take a look at some of these popular Aztec tales that hold some significance and are retold to date.

The Creation of Music

On one beautiful day, when the wind was blowing, and the birds were chirping, the sky god,

Tezcatlipoca, and the wind god, Quetzalcoatl, met on a wild plain. While they helped each other in times of crisis, they also got into little tiffs now and then. On that day, Tezcatlipoca arrived first and waited for Quetzalcoatl to get there. Impatient, he asked Quetzalcoatl the reason for his late arrival. To this, Quetzalcoatl replied, "I've been extremely busy due to the hurricane season." However, Tezcatlipoca completely ignored his argument and replied, "Listen to me, there are much more serious problems than this," to which the wind god replied, "I am not sure about that."

Tezcatlipoca calmly replied, "Hear me out. Take a moment and look around. Do you hear anything?" "No, nothing," replied Quetzalcoatl. "That's what I have been saying," ranted Tezcatlipoca. "Nothing! No one whispers, talks, or sings. No one plays too. We only get to hear you shouting, screaming, and roaring. This cannot go on for long. We need to wake everyone up, not by means of your wind roar or hurricane sounds but through music. We should have music!" Surprised and now in deep thought, Quetzalcoatl replied, "I don't know how I can help you with this. I have no music or source to create it."

"I know who can help us," exclaimed Tezcatli-poca. "The Sun has plenty of musicians and singers who surround him all day. They entertain him and sing for him when he is bored. However, he never shares the music with anyone." "I think this is unfair on us and everyone," replied Quetzalcoatl. The sky god then urged Quetzalcoatl to travel to the sun's house and pick the best artists and musicians. With this, the wind god began his quest to wake up the living beings and the world.

Quetzalcoatl flew day and night, covering miles and miles to reach the sun's house. He kept his eyes open to spot a beach over the endless horizons. Upon spotting one, he took a break and pleaded with the gods for help. He specifically called the three servants of God- Water Woman, Cane and Conch, and Water Monster to help him cover the remaining distance and reach the sun. The three servants came together to form an intertwined rope and make a long bridge to cover the distance. The rope grew longer and eventually disappeared into heaven. Quetzalcoatl hopped on the bridge and followed it until he reached the sky.

Upon arrival, the wind god had to go through a confusing maze of streets that led him to the sun's house. However, the journey was not easy as it even took him some time to find the entrance. He was tired and ready to give up. After a while, he heard a beautiful melody from a distance. Assuming that it came from the sun's house, Quetzalcoatl followed the tune and reached the house's courtyard. He realized that the melody was extremely soothing, light, sweet, and cool during his journey. "So this is music!" exclaimed Quetzalcoatl to himself.

He stood in the courtyard and scanned the musicians from top to bottom, slyly savoring the sweet melody. He noticed that every group was allotted different outfits with varied hues that set them apart. For instance, blue outfits were worn by the wandering minstrels, golden yellow dresses marked the flute players, red outfits were provided to the singers, and white was the color of the lullaby singers. Upon seeing Quetzalcoatl in his court, the Sun panicked and demanded the musicians stop playing. He feared them being taken to the silent universe again. However, Quetzalcoatl commanded them to go with him under the influence of the sky god.

At first, the sun and the musicians ignored him, which angered Quetzalcoatl. His roars and screams exploded into thunder and hurricane. The sky turned black, and dark clouds surrounded the sun's house. Fearing Quetzalcoatl's wrath, the musicians sat in his lap and agreed to go with him. Quetzalcoatl's anger instantly vanished, and he felt proud carrying the musicians home. As he approached the earth, a new sensation and feeling swirled throughout the land. New flowers bloomed, and fruits ripened as they heard sweet music spreading in their world.

Animals, humans, and plants seemed to awaken from a long slumber. The musicians played melodies that reached deep into the forests, oceans, and valleys. Every creature then learned to dance, sing, and play. The musicians were happy to spread the joy and called this world their new home. To date, we can listen to the pleasant harmonies of leaves rustling through the wind or birds chirping in the morning.

The Discovery of Corn

When Quetzalcoatl was allotted the task of making humans to create a new world, he had to reach the underworld to gather bones hidden by Mictlante-cuhtli, the God of Death. However, it was not an easy feat as Mictlantecuhtli ordered Quetzalcoatl to go through a few tests before he could have the bones. Even though Quetzalcoatl passed his tests, the death god cheated and refused to give up the bones. This urged Quetzalcoatl to steal them and flee. However, he was captured by Mictlantecuht-li's helpers. The bones he held broke after falling on the ground. Quetzalcoatl then collected the broken bones and managed to escape. Once he reached Ta-moanchan (gods' paradise), he took help from Ci-huacóatl, who ground the bones. Quetzalcoatl then sprinkled his own blood on the ground bones to create life.

Even though the humans were created in accu-rate proportions and were alive, Quetzalcoatl no-ticed signs of floundering and weakness. He real-ized that they needed food to sustain their health. He sought to discover food for the humans after consulting other gods and animals. They decided to help Quetzalcoatl and sought to find food. After a while, the red ant reached atop Tonacatépetl (the Mountain of Our Sustenance) and found a few corn kernels. He offered the kernels to humans, which impressed Quetzalcoatl. Even though the red ant wanted to keep the location a secret, Quetzalcoatl pressured him to reveal the location of the food.

The ant also offered a few kernels to the gods after turning black. The gods ate the corn and chewed on them vigorously to turn the food into a paste. Eventually, the paste was collected and placed on the humans' lips to give them strength and get them on their feet. To get more grains from Tonacatépetl, Quetzalcoatl used strong ropes to drag the hill. However, his unsuccessful attempts led Nanáhuatl and the Tlaloques (the Gods of the Rain) to split it open. The kernels flooded the ground and took the colors that represented the Tlaloques- white, blue, red, and yellow. Other food items that fell from the mountain were chia, amaranth, beans, and fish amaranth. In turn, the humans had provision of food and multiple options to choose from. They fed on the grains to gain nutrition and grow stronger.

The Rag-Picker and the Priest

A Nahua rag-picker worked at the famous temple, Huitzilopochtli, to earn food and his daily wages. One day when working, he stumbled across a painted book that mysteriously lay on the ground. Unable to decipher it, the rag-picker took the book to a priest to decode the text. The priest revealed that the book directed them to find a magical casket buried deep in the pyramid. One could only find it if they reached the ninety-third step of the structure. Excited, they hurried to the pyramid and agreed to split the rewards. Once they reached the 93rd step, they put in all their strength to lift the stone to find the casket.

As expected, they found a casket surrounded by a shiny chain. They opened the casket and found a few magical items; a future-showing mirror, a sorcery book, a magic wand, a drumstick and rattle, and an almanac. The priest convinced the rag-picker to give him the entire casket with all items in exchange for 300 gold pieces. The priest insisted that the rag-picker would misuse the magical items and decided to be their sole owner. Once the rag-picker received his gold, he hit the priest on his head using the wand. He picked up the magical items, threw the priest in the lake, and hurried home.

He was curious to learn more about the items and wanted to use them to become powerful. However, he failed to decipher the almanac and misused the mirror. He was scared when he shook the rattle and could not understand the sounds it made. He felt a strange presence around him and feared the noise of spirits. Eventually, the rag-picker concluded that the magical things were a curse and decided to throw them in the river. He was extremely scared and feared being possessed by bad spirits. The next day, he woke up and approached the lake where he threw the priest's body. With a heavy heart, he threw the casket packed with the magical things in the lake, expecting this to diminish his grief and allow him to live peacefully again.

As soon as the casket touched the water, the priest appeared in front of him, alive. He grabbed the casket and got hold of the magic wand. He used it to hit the rag-picker's head and kill him. The priest then dragged the casket along and buried it in a safe place such that no one could find and misuse it.

This story teaches us about the price one must pay when he becomes extremely greedy and fails to consider the consequences of his actions.

Journey of a Princess

In the past, the Aztecs would usually go to war to feed the gods but stopped once they settled on "The Place of the Prickly Pear Cactus" (a magical island that appears in another Aztec tale). Ancient myths say that the Aztecs stopped going to war following the gods' order. They were meant to stay in one place and regain their strength. Instead of sacrificing their captives, they now had to use their own group members as a sacrifice to the gods as they still needed to feed them. Once they settled in and established their base on the island, the Aztec emperor decided to find a bride for his son and continue the legacy.

He sent an invitation to a princess of their neighboring tribe and asked her to meet his son. The princess accepted the invitation and reached the island with several servants who carried presents for the Aztec emperor's family. The prince and princess met and shared a delightful dinner.

She was pleased with the prince's etiquettes and agreed to marry him. The princess lived in the Aztec capital for a few days until the wedding date arrived. Later, when her father visited the capital, he was shocked to learn that the princess and her servants were sacrificed to the gods. This angered the chief, who then declared war against the Aztecs. He was not able to accept that being sacrificed was an honor.

As the chief's army arrived at the Aztec capital, both sides entered a dreadful war. However, as the Aztec gods suggested the community stay put and gather their strength, most of them were extremely capable of fighting and gathered enough weapons to defeat the enemies. When they won, they asked for captives, food, and jewels to sustain their livelihood and feed their gods. Over time, they conquered every neighboring region and expanded their community, thereby becoming one of the richest tribes there.

The Legend of Chocolate

The Toltecs, a tribe, vaguely linked to the Aztecs, were not as rich as the Aztecs and suffered from hunger and poverty. They hunted for food day and night but failed to grow and cook their findings, which intensified their suffering. The gods took pity and decided to send Quetzalcoatl to grow and cook food. One morning when Quetzalcoatl descended on the land, the Toltecs spotted him in a flash of light that appeared as a dot. They saw a human figure approaching them and feared him due to his peculiar silhouette and special powers. They assumed him to be superhuman and began worshipping him.

The Toltecs decided to replan their city, Tollan, and build a mansion for the superhuman in the center. They carved the pillars into intricate human shapes and added a grand staircase in the entrance. The tribe used the best quality materials and stones found in their region. Upon seeing this, Quetzalcoatl invited Tlaloc and his wife, Xochiquetzal, to descend to the earth and live with him. During their time on the land, the three good gods taught the Toltecs to grow their own food, farm, and cook the product to perfection. Over time, the people could grow nutritious food and cook healthy meals, which helped them gain strength and overcome their misery.

The gods also taught the people to look at the stars and study them to keep their lives on track. Some of them became artists and astronomers. They made their own calendars and learned to read the dates and mark the seasons. The gods helped them highlight the dates and periods of optimum harvest and seed planting. The Toltecs steadily expanded their base and grew multiple grains and food items such as maize, yucca, beans, vegetables, and fruits.

Before Quetzalcoatl stepped on earth, he sneakily brought a cocoa plant owned by his twin brother, who wanted to save the plant for himself and other gods. He felt that humans did not deserve the products and juice of this plant. However, Quetzalcoatl thought otherwise. When the Toltecs finally learned to farm and grow their own food without being dependent on others, Quetzalcoatl decided that it was time to give them the cocoa plant. The plant was beautiful to look at as the bright green leaves hung low on its branches.

With the help of Tlaloc, Quetzalcoatl planted it and asked Tlaloc to make it rain. Furthermore, Xochiquetzal was asked to use her special powers to provide proper nutrition to the soil and grow flowers on the plant. With the grace of the three gods, the cocoa plant grew healthy on an attractive farm. The gods and the people waited for the flowers to bloom and the fruits to sprout. Once they did, the little pods were collected and toasted by Quetzalcoatl. The Toltecs learned how to separate the seeds and use the gourds to make the precious drink.

In the beginning, the drink extracted from the cocoa plant was extremely bitter, which was later sweetened using honey. Due to the rarity of this plant, only the priest, nobles, and individuals with higher ranks were allowed to drink its juice. After some time, the Spanish conquered the region; they heated the drink and mixed it with sugar and milk. They savored its taste, and cocoa soon became famous and valuable. Traders conducted business using cocoa in exchange for goods. This made the gods angry and swore to avenge this secrecy. They approached the God of Darkness, Texcatlipoca, who was Quetzalcoatl's enemy.

Tezcatlipoca descended on the land disguised as a spider and entered Quetzalcoatl's palace without leaving a trace. Quetzalcoatl somehow figured out what was happening as he had consecutive nightmares about angry gods and their evil acts of revenge on him. More importantly, he was more worried about the people of his region. Tezcatlipoca waited for the right time to meet Quetzalcoatl and take revenge. One day, he transformed into a trader dealing in pulque drinks and offered one to Quetzalcoatl. They raised a toast to a happy and prosperous life and wished a peaceful future for the Toltecs. As Quetzalcoatl chugged his drink, he saw Texcatlipoca exhibiting an evil smile and immediately began dancing and singing. He was unaware of his acts and passed out completely.

When Quetzalcoatl opened his eyes, he realized what happened and instantly felt embarrassed. He let the Toltecs down and learned that they had gone back to their hardships and miserable lives. He saw the dried farms and lifeless cocoa plants around him. He felt embarrassed and decided to run away in the direction of the evening star. He ran and ran until he reached the western beaches. He took a break and planted the leftover cocoa seeds into the land. This is why cocoa plants are grown in hot and tropical regions today. In a way, the Aztecs believe that the earth was blessed with chocolate due to the acts of Quetzalcoatl.

While there are numerous other tales told under the Aztec label, the ones we went through are the most popular and coveted, especially among children.

Chapter 5:

Traditions and Customs

The traditions and customs followed by the Aztecs were predominantly dictated by the myths and beliefs of the past. In a way, they were influenced by the superstitions and ancient mythology passed on by their ancestors. In this chapter, we will cover some significant traditions and customs followed by the Aztecs that were heavily influenced by Aztec mythology.

Customs in Daily Life

The religious and customary practices of the Aztecs were altered over time and changed by scholars and priests every few years. Irrespective of the changes, the cultures that thrived were extremely rich and favored by the tribes. For the Aztecs, prayer and work were the two main customary domains of everyday life. They put education above all and ensured proper knowledge and learning for their children. Along with this, the male students were also sent to receive military education. Tasks like buying goods and trading were assigned to the men, whereas the women were asked to manage the household. However, they had the freedom to engage in outdoor activities as much as they liked.

The religious beliefs of this community stemmed from their ancestors and their tales about the Aztec gods. Religious worship, rituals, and prayers formed a significant part of the holy customs and major fields of life. While the priests in temples and religious leaders were given importance, the common man would also conduct prayer at his home in front of a shrine (every household had a shrine at that time). Along with daily praying, some men and women also held fasts to impress the gods. Since there were multiple gods, goddesses, and deities of the Aztecs, the community was divided on the basis of a polytheistic set of rituals and beliefs. Human sacrifice and military quests formed an integral part of their belief system, which also connected the gods to the humans.

Other popular customs included dancing, singing, and taking psychoactive drugs during important religious festivals. Since the Aztecs had unique thoughts on the afterlife and death, they would take the act of burials and rites seriously. They ensured that the dead were honorably buried for a chance to live peacefully in their new life. Some even considered cremating the bodies instead of burying them, as the souls were believed to go to heaven.

Customs for the Noble and Peasants

The emperors and nobles were considered the children of the deities, which made them next to Godly. The Aztecs had to respect this belief and allow special privileges for the emperors. This also gave birth to a rigid communal hierarchy that put the nobles on a pedestal. They were exempt from following the laws and could wear any clothing of their choice. On the other hand, the commoners were not allowed to wear jewelry and distinct kinds of clothing. The kids of the royal family were also given private schooling as opposed to the children of the commoners who attended public schools.

Moreover, the slaves and peasants followed a set of rituals and customs similar to the European serfs of that time. While most peasants were appointed to harvest the kings' lands and farm, some of them were sold to merchants or other royal families, particularly those appointed to work on specific pieces of land. They had the freedom to marry if they wanted but had no say when their children were sold off too. As mentioned, cremating a dead body was considered holy as the act could send the body to heaven. However, only people of royal families and higher stature had access to this. The peasants, slaves, and commoners were mostly buried after death.

Significant Traditions

The Aztecs followed seven holy traditions that were extracted from their mythology and ancient tales. They are as follows:

1. New Fire Ceremony

As mentioned earlier, the New Fire Ceremony was conducted once an entire cycle of the calendar was completed, once every 52 years. While myths say that this tradition began in 1090, some claim it to be of ancient origin. This tradition was carried out until the Spanish invaded the region, which was in 1507. As the cycle neared its end, the Aztecs would start preparing for the ceremony, presumably during the last five days. They would clean the house, get rid of clutter, fast, cleanse, rest, and practice silence. A man would be chosen as a sacrifice to the gods. He was taken atop a mountain where the holy fire was lit.

2. Human Sacrifice

As mentioned throughout the book, human sacrifice was an important religious ritual of this community. Mesoamerica held a long record of sacrificing humans, which involved the Zapotecs and the Mayans. The Aztecs believed that the gods jumped into the fire to create humans, which is why human sacrifice is their duty and offering. The Aztecs wanted to repay the debt, and one person was chosen at the end of each cycle. This also led to the practice of self-sacrifice, where some people would cut their ears, tongues, or genitals, offering the blood to the gods. The Aztecs would also sacrifice animals by slaughtering them. Humans were sacrificed by carving their hearts out. The skins, bones, and skulls of the victims were displayed as gods' relics. Some were even used in oracles and ritual masks.

3. Ullamaliztli- Aztec Ball Game

The rules and concepts of this game can be traced back to the time of the Olmec civilization. While the game was mainly played for entertainment, some added in religious and political angles, which is why it grew more popular. Huitzilopochtli was given a new altar by the Aztecs, who also built an adjacent ball court on their new settlement. The walls had six markers and an "I"-shaped court in the center that was divided by a centerline. The judges, nobles, and other spectators were seated on the sides.

The players were supplied with protective equipment and given a 9-pound ball known as "Olli" to play with. They had to pass the ball to other team members without letting it touch the ground. They would score points if they successfully let the ball pass through a stone ring. The player who made the winning shot could carry the public's blankets home, which resulted in a heated game with the crowd screaming and placing multiple bets on the best players. While royal families and nobles would bet large sums of money and cities, the poor would put their food on the table. Some even bet their freedom and turned into slaves after losing.

4. Rain Festivals

The month of February was marked as the beginning of the farmer's year when the Aztecs conducted the rain festival. A shaman or priest was appointed to chant a set of holy affirmations and mantras to please the rain gods and welcome rain. As March arrived and the flowers bloomed, the Aztecs conducted another rain festival to call Tlaloc and seek blessings. The third festival was celebrated during the fall season when they called Tlaloc again. However, the third celebration included images and mountain forms of Tlaloc as he was believed to reside in a mountain.

5. Poetry and Songs

The Aztecs loved songs, poetry, and prose. They held poetry contests and encouraged people to participate in them. The winners were rewarded handsomely and praised for their creativity. Some of these contests and competitions also included presentations and shows by musicians, acrobats, and artists. While some contests were held independently, most of them would be a part of the Aztec festivals. Some famous songs and their versions included Teocuitlatl (for myths and gods), Yaocuicatl (for war), and Xochicuicatl (for poetry and flowers). You can still find different versions of preconquest poems of the Aztecs today.

6. Xilonen Festival

Xilonen, the corn goddess, was paid tribute during this festival. Young and single girls were asked to let their hair loose and keep it long. They would also participate in long processions toward the temple and carry green corn as an offering. Every year, a slave would dress like this Goddess by putting on an outfit. This festival was celebrated over a few days, with the last day dedicated to sacrificing the slave.

7. The Cocoa Bean and Chocolate

As you previously learned, the cocoa bean and chocolate were extremely significant to the Aztecs as the God Quetzalcoatl first brought it to earth and planted it for the locals to cherish. Before milk was used regularly, the Aztecs added spices, corn-flour, and chilies to the chocolate drink to enhance its taste. Chocolate was called "chocolatl" in the language of the Aztecs and has since become significant to the community.

Traditional Foods of the Aztecs

The Aztecs considered corn, meats, chilies, beans, honey, and chocolate as traditional and staple foods, as most of them were believed to be granted by the gods. Their main dishes included maize porridge, honey, chilies, sauce, beans, and tortillas. They ate only twice a day, once after waking up and the second time around 3 in the afternoon (or any other hottest hour of the day). Lunch included beans, tamales, tomato and squash casserole, and tortillas. These ingredients were also used during religious feasts that were held as per the Aztec calendar. Consuming hallucinogenic mushrooms and tobacco was also a custom and an integral part of the religious festivities.

Since maize was often mentioned in Aztec mythology, the community considered it to be an important grain of ancient significance. Over time, they planted corn in major areas to feed the entire community. An alkaline solution was used to soak and cook dry maize for consumption. The Aztecs grew this precious grain in various textures, qualities, sizes, and colors. Some were even ground to make flour and produce tortillas, maize gruel, or tamales. A range of vegetables and fruits, including squash, tomatoes, avocados, onions, sweet potatoes, and chili peppers, were also grown.

Conclusion

As mentioned at the beginning of the book, ancient Aztec mythology had a heavy impact on the community, which can be noted to date. In a way, technological advancements and innovations stem from ancient beliefs and myths. We can witness this through the way the Aztecs built structures and capital cities for their gods. The knowledge and strength to take up these massive projects were supposedly provided by the gods, which spurred the Aztecs into completing the construction within short periods of time. The innovative ideas, creativity, and other constructive qualities were passed on to the following generations.

Such an influential power was noted in just one other version of mythology, Greek. Ancient Aztec and Greek myths cover society's respect for creativity, innovation, and productivity, allowing communities and neighboring civilizations to grow their base and modify their environments. For instance, Tenochtitlan, the capital city of the Aztecs, was solely extracted from their myth. It is believed that the city's founders were guided by the god Huitzilopochtli who whispered the directions in their ears. When they reached Lake Texcoco, they were forced to fight Huitzilopochtli's nephew, Copil. However, the humans won with the help of Huitzilopochtli's idol that they carried along. They threw Copil's heart in the lake and marked the spot as the new capital city. In a way, the Aztecs followed the gods' whims to extend their innovative power.

As they developed the city and agricultural lands around them, they also constructed floating gardens or "chinampas" to extend their infrastructure. With architectural creativity and technological innovations, the Aztecs also continued to worship the gods and reframed their beliefs based on the changes made in their myth. The polytheistic religious beliefs were somehow shattered after the Spanish conquered the region. However, the Mexicans still hold on to their own version of mythology and take pride in the strong cultural implications that were adapted until now.

References

An Aztec Legend. (n.d.). Retrieved from Native-languages.org website: http://www.native-languages.org/aztecstory.htm

aprilholloway. (n.d.). Aztec creation myths. Retrieved from Ancient-origins.net website: https://www.ancient-origins.net/human-origins-folklore/aztec-creation-myths-0071

Aztec Creation Story. (n.d.). Retrieved from Uintahbasintah.org website: http://www.uintah-basintah.org/csaztec.htm

Aztec Customs. (n.d.). Retrieved from Aztecsandtenochtitlan.com website: https://aztecsand-tenochtitlan.com/aztec-civilisation/aztec-customs/

Aztec story for kids - journey of a princess - Aztecs for kids. (n.d.). Retrieved from Mrdonn.org website: https://aztecs.mrdonn.org/princess. html

Calhoun, C. (2012, March 23). The legend of chocolate: Origin story and hot chocolate recipe. Retrieved from Delishably website: https:// delishably.com/desserts/legend-of-chocolate

Chao-Fong, L. (2020a, February 3). The 8 most important gods and goddesses of the Aztec empire. Retrieved from History Hit website: https://www.historyhit.com/most-important-gods-and-goddesses-of-the-aztec-empire

Chao-Fong, L. (2020b, February 3). What did the Aztecs eat and drink? Mexican food of the middle ages. Retrieved from History Hit website: https://www.historyhit.com/mexican-food-of-the-middle-ages-what-did-the-az-tecs-eat-and-drink/

Goodwin, M. F. (2017, September 25). The 7 traditions and customs of the most outstanding Aztecs. Retrieved from Lifepersona.com website: https://www.lifepersona.com/the-7-traditions-and-customs-of-the-most-outstanding-aztecs

Lessner, J. (2020, September 1). These are the top 11 gods and goddesses of the Aztec empire that you should know about. Retrieved from Wearemitu.com website: https://wearemitu. com/culture/these-are-the-top-11-gods-and-goddesses-of-the-aztec-empire-that-you-should-know-about/

Maestri, N. (n.d.-a). Centeotl. from Thoughtco. com website: https://www.thoughtco.com/ centeotl-the-aztec-god-of-maize-170309

Maestri, N. (n.d.-b). Important Aztec gods and goddesses. Retrieved from Thoughtco.com website: https://www.thoughtco.com/dei-ties-of-mexica-mythology-170042

Maestri, N. (n.d.-c). The legend of the fifth sun. Retrieved from Thoughtco.com website: https://www.thoughtco.com/aztec-cre-ation-myth-169337

Maestri, N. (n.d.-d). Who was the Aztec Goddess of maguey and pulque? Retrieved from Thought-co.com   website: https://www.thoughtco. com/mayahuel-the-aztec-goddess-of-ma-guey-171570

Micky Bumbar (Lords of the Drinks). (2015, May 13). The Aztec myth of the 400 drunken rabbit Gods explains all levels of intoxication. Retrieved from Lordsofthedrinks.com website: https://lordsofthedrinks.com/2015/05/13/the-aztec-myth-of-the-400-drunken-rabbit-gods-explains-all-levels-of-intoxication/

Monsters of Aztec mythology. (n.d.). Retrieved from Fandom.com website: https://campaztecroleplaying.fandom.com/wiki/Monsters_of_Aztec_Mythology

Ortíz, A. (2021, March 10). Learn about Mexican history through its mythical world. Retrieved from Xcaret.com website: https://blog.xcaret.com/en/mythological-creatures-mexico/